Fiona the Firefly

Story and Illustrations by
Wendy Connelly

Ambassador Books, Inc.
Worcester • Massachusetts

Library of Congress Cataloging-in-Publication Data

Connelly, Wendy, 1980-
  Fiona the firefly! / by Wendy Connelly.
      p. cm.
Summary: Fiona, a bug who sees nothing special in herself, finds that her beautiful actions come to be reflected in her physical appearance.
  ISBN 1-929039-16-6 (hardcover)
 [1. Self-perception--Fiction. 2. Fireflies--Fiction. 3. Insects--Fiction.
      4. Stories in rhyme.] I. Title.

  PZ8.3.C764Fi 2003
  [E]--dc22
                                2003015195

Published in 2003 in the United States by Ambassador Books, Inc.
91 Prescott Street, Worcester, Massachusetts 01605
(800) 577-0909

For current information about all titles from Ambassador Books, Inc. visit our website at:
www.ambassadorbooks.com.

Printed in China.

Dedication

In loving memory of Shane Luksa:
Your light still glows in our hearts.

Your light must shine before others that they may see
your good deeds and glorify your heavenly Father.
— *Matthew 5: 15-16*

Fiona the Bug let out a long sigh,
"I'm not very special. I can't fly too high.

"My wings cannot match
Belle Butterfly's splendor.

"I cannot weave webs
like Spider the Spinner.

"I'm not hip or trendy like Ladybug Dot.

"I cannot make honey . . .

. . . like Bee Buzz-a-lot."

But Fiona the Bug was determined to find
her own special beauty, her own way to shine,
And a bright idea popped into her mind . . .

"I can be kind and help bugs in need
And brighten the day with a simple good deed."

So whenever an insect
was caught up in trouble,

Fiona the Bug was
there on the double!

She plopped in a puddle
to rescue Beetle Bob.

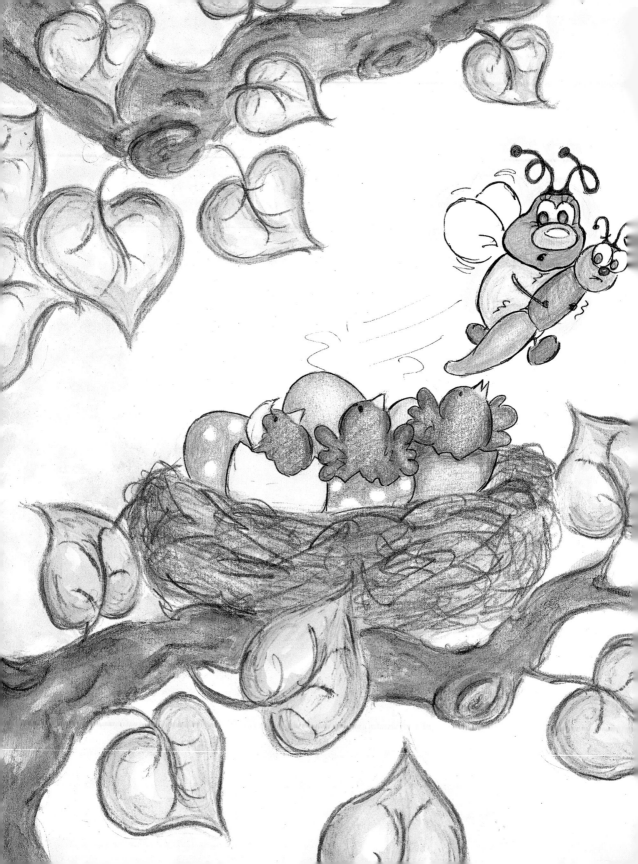

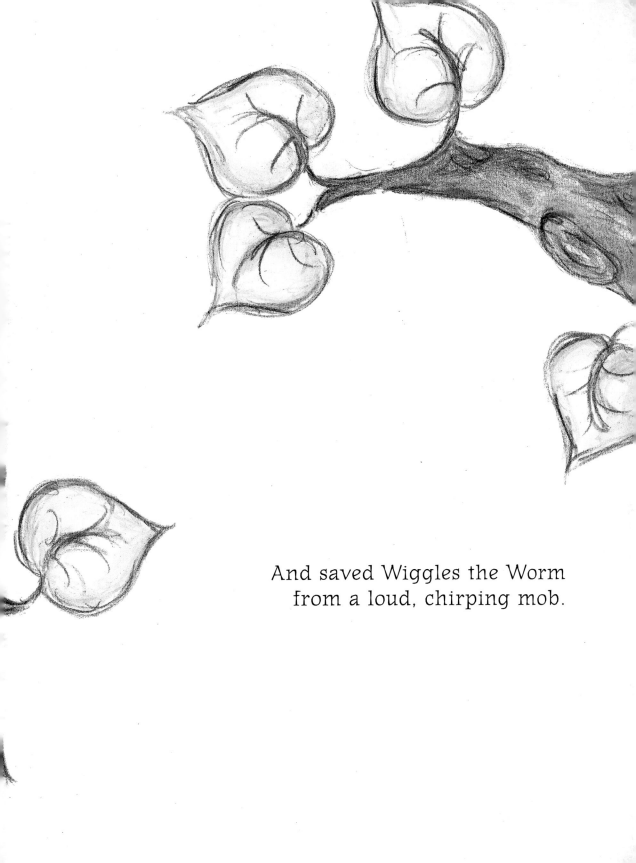

And saved Wiggles the Worm
from a loud, chirping mob.

When elderly ants were crossing the road,
Fiona was there to lighten their load.

With every small kindness she lit up within,

And that's when her talent could truly begin.

Fiona the Bug grew fiery and bright,
for nothing could dim her beautiful light.

Although her kind acts were never for show,
the other bugs noticed her radiant glow.

And deep in her heart the little bug knew
she had a bright gift that made her special, too.

She razzled and dazzled
as she buzzed through the sky,

For Fiona the Bug was a bright firefly!

Fiona the Bug learned a very important lesson. It doesn't matter what we look like or where we come from. What matters is how we act. When we love others and help them, the light of God's love shines in us. It makes others happy and it makes us happy, too.